Cameron's Dinosaur Band

Written by
Stephanie L. Schultz

Characters designed by
Michael J. Schultz

Illustrated by **iNDOS Studio**

This book is for children of all ages. Never stop trying to do what you love.

This book is dedicated to my family

I'm especially grateful to Uncle Michael for taking
the time to create such lovable characters.

And special thanks to Uncle David who provided
considerable resources to bring this
book to completion.

This is Cameron. She's five.

Cameron is excited this morning because her babysitter, AJ, is coming. When Cameron and AJ draw pictures together, amazing things happen!

Today Cameron wants to draw
dinosaurs. She and her brother play
with dinosaur toys and they like to
draw them, too. Cameron sets crayons
and a pad of paper on the floor.
She begins to draw.

The doorbell rings. Cameron squeals, "It's AJ!" When AJ enters the room with Cameron's mother, Cameron hugs her babysitter hello. Cameron's mother smiles and gives Cameron a kiss before she leaves.

"What are you drawing?" AJ asks. Cameron sounds excited. "It's a T-Rex! My favorite!" "Great work," says AJ as Cameron fills in the last spot of the dinosaur's blue skin.

After a few minutes, Cameron looks up from her paper. "It's too quiet. Can you please put music on?" AJ finds her phone and with a few taps, music fills the room.

The sounds make Cameron twirl and ask, "What's this music?" AJ replies, "It's jazz! Do you like it?" AJ knows Cameron likes the jazz because she doesn't stop dancing. AJ spreads a large piece of paper on the coffee table then begins to draw.

Still spinning, Cameron circles closer to AJ and asks, "What are you making?" When she sees AJ's drawing, she gets an idea. "Hey, they can be a band. A dinosaur band!" Cameron holds up her picture of the blue T-Rex. She asks, "What instrument can she play?"

AJ answers, "Well, Cameron, let's think. Close your eyes. What instruments do you hear?"

As Cameron shuts her eyes to listen, she lets the music carry her away.

When she lifts her eyelids, Cameron sees the blue T-Rex towering over her. Cameron looks around. She is not in her living room anymore, she's in a big park. With a knowing smile, Cameron thinks, "AJ!" Cameron blinks in the sunlight and says to the T-Rex, "Hello, there! What's your name?" The T-Rex answers, "My name is Trane. These sounds are wonderful, let's follow them to learn what they are."

The jazz is still playing. Far ahead they see a stage where colorful dinosaurs are playing instruments of many shapes and sizes. Cameron points to the stage. "It's coming from over there! Let's go!"

The stream of sound grows louder as Cameron races toward the dinosaurs. Taking great leaps, Trane follows closely behind.

They stop short when they reach the stage.
The music feels even more amazing up close,
and for several minutes they just listen
and watch. Some of the instruments are new to
her, but Cameron is happy to see one dinosaur
sitting at a piano that looks like the one
she is learning to play. She also recognizes
drums, and a trumpet like the one
that belongs to her brother.

The jazz is making Cameron dance again. She wishes she could make this music.
Cameron can see that her new friend feels the same way.

Suddenly, the band is quiet. A dinosaur with a long neck and a large instrument resting on its shoulder calls out. "Look! We have an audience!" Cameron is very still. She says softly, "Uh, my name is Cameron and this is my friend Trane." Trane is excited and asks, "Can I play?"

An orange dinosaur with a trumpet asks Trane,
"What instrument do you play?" Trane says,
"I don't have one, I've never played an instrument.
But I love your music!" "Well," says the orange
dinosaur, "love is the most important thing,
so you are on your way."

The orange dinosaur walks to the edge of the stage and says to Trane, "My name is Miles. We're taking a break. Why don't you give this a try?" Miles lifts the shining trumpet to his mouth to show Trane what to do, then holds it out to her.

Trane takes the trumpet from Miles, but her thick fingers get stuck as she tries to press the tiny buttons. She sighs and wonders what else she might try.

Seeing Trane's problem, the dinosaur at the piano calls out, "Hi there! My name is Red. Your fingers will fit this piano. Come try it!"

But Trane is disappointed again.
Her nose hits the top of the instrument
before her arms reach the keys.

Cameron looks at the dinosaur who spoke to them first. This dinosaur is holding an instrument that looks like a giant violin. Cameron is sure this instrument is a better fit for Trane. Cameron looks at the dinosaur hopefully. The dinosaur nods her head. She will let Trane try her bass.

The dinosaur waves. "Hi, Trane. I'm Chambers. Come try my bass." Chambers rests the bass on Trane's shoulder. It's tall and light and Trane feels comfortable until she tries to press the narrow strings. "Ugh!" She is frustrated again. "My fingers are also too large for the bass!"

Cameron looks around at the band.
She sees the drums and knows Trane won't
fit behind those, so she says nothing. Then
she sees a purple dinosaur and shouts,
"Let's ask about that instrument!"

Cameron walks up to this unusual purple dinosaur. "Hello! I'm Cameron, and this is my friend, Trane. Can she borrow your instrument?"

The dinosaur's voice is bright when he says,
"Sure Trane! Try this tenor saxophone.
And please, call me Sonny."
Sonny rests the saxophone in Trane's hands
and watches her blow into the mouthpiece.
The saxophone makes a loud honk.
The noise does not sound like music,
but Trane is delighted.

Miles steps to the front of the stage and says cheerfully, "I knew you would find the right instrument. That's how my trumpet sounded the first time I tried it. I got better with practice, and you will too."

Cameron is filled with joy as the band starts to play again. She wraps her arms tightly around Trane and moves with the music until she falls backwards onto... the couch in her living room!

Just then, Cameron's mother enters the room. At first Cameron is surprised to feel the sofa under her bottom, but then she smiles.

Cameron's mother asks, "Did you have fun while I was away?" Cameron looks at AJ and says to her mother, "Yes! We drew pictures and listened to jazzy music and I learned that if you really want to do something, you should never give up!" "That sounds great, I'm glad you had fun!" says Cameron's mother. "Now say goodbye to AJ. You'll see her again soon."

Cameron gives AJ a squeeze.

She giggles and says, "See you next time!"

THE END

About the Creative Team

As an author, Stephanie Schultz is inspired
by people, especially the children she babysits
for and by her incredibly loving, talented
and generous family.

Michael Schultz has been entertaining others
for decades with his witty caricatures.